Echoes of The Twins

By India Cunningham

Words 17,053

Dedication

First, I want to thank *me* for believing in myself yes, I had to get that out! To my family, thank you for supporting my dreams, even during the times when I doubted myself. It's been a long journey, and I'm deeply grateful for your unwavering love and encouragement over the years. I love you all from the bottom of my heart.

A special thank you goes to my therapist, Ms. Chen. If you're reading this, I want you to know how much I appreciate your guidance and encouragement. You believed in me when I struggled to believe in myself, and your words about giving life to stiff bones truly resonated with me. I'm forever grateful for the impact of our sessions together.

Finally, to my readers and supporters: thank you for embracing this book. I know it's a bit different from what you're used to, especially when it comes to themes like Yin and Yang, but I wanted to try something new, and it worked! Your love and enthusiasm mean the world to me. Thank you for taking this journey with me.

With love and gratitude,
India Cunningham

Introduction

The universe hummed with creation. Galaxies spun like pinwheels of light, their colors swirling in a dance choreographed by unseen forces. At the center of it all were Yin and Yang two beings of infinite power, bound by their duality yet driven by contrasting desires.

Yin, the elder, embodied stillness and contemplation. She found solace in observing the worlds she had shaped, marveling at the intricate lives of the beings that thrived within them. Yang, on the other hand, was restless. She craved motion, discovery, and the chaos that came with stepping into the unknown.

You never tire of watching, Yang said one day, her golden eyes alight with curiosity as she gazed through the shimmering portal that displayed the realms they had crafted. "But what if there's more than just observing? What if we *lived* it?

Yin frowned, her silver gaze steady and calm. What would we gain by stepping into what we already know? These realms are ours, Yang. We shaped them. They exist because of us.

But we don't *know* them, Yang countered. Her voice was alive with conviction. Not really. What if there's something out there something even, we can't imagine?

Reluctantly, Yin turned her attention to the portal Yang was so fixated on. It revealed a realm teeming with life, marked by the imperfections and complexities that made it unique. Among its many beings was a planet Earth. Its denizens fascinated Yang, their emotions raw and unguarded, their lives fleeting yet full of purpose.

I want to go there, Yang declared, pointing to Earth.

Yin hesitated. To leave their home would mean abandoning their omnipotence, severing their connection to the cosmos they had created. It was a leap into uncertainty, a choice that could unravel everything they knew.

Yang... Yin began, her voice heavy with warning.

But Yang was already reaching for her hand. Please, she whispered. Come with me. Let's find out what it means to truly *be*.

Against her better judgment, Yin relented.

And so, the twins leaped into the unknown, leaving behind their celestial throne for a world that would test the limits of their bond, their power, and their very existence. They arrived as strangers in a strange land, unaware of the trials awaiting them.

As their feet touched the soil of Earth, they could feel their connection to their cosmic origins fading. The weight of mortality settled on their shoulders, and for the first time, they were no longer creators but participants in a story they had yet to understand.

What neither twin knew was that their arrival would spark a chain of events that would forever alter the balance of the universe starting with a single, ordinary high school on Earth.

Yin & Yang Interlude

(Lights fade in, revealing a cosmic expanse star glimmering softly, an ethereal world in endless creation. Yin sits at a floating desk, surrounded by orbs of swirling light, deep in thought. Yang paces restlessly nearby, eyes alight with curiosity and mischief.)

Yang: (sighs dramatically) Hey, Yin, what are you up to?

Yin: (without looking up) Hmm, not much. Just contemplating what to create next. I'm in one of those thinking moods.

Yang: (groaning) Ugh, I'm bored. There's nothing left for us to do here! We've created everything we could possibly create. I need something new, something exciting.

Yin: (glancing up, unimpressed) Exciting? What do you mean? We've got everything we need right here. What could be more exciting than this?

Yang: (gesturing wildly) I don't know... Maybe exploring some of the realms we've made! I've been watching them, Yin. Some of them have potential. There are beings in their creatures who might surprise us.

Yin: (shrugging, uninterested) I don't know, Yang. Those realms are fine. We created them, gave life to the beings there. But I'm happy staying here. Watching them evolve from a distance is enough. Why do you want to go there?

Yang: (stepping closer, eyes sparkling) Because it's different! This one realm look at it! (waves a hand, revealing a shimmering portal) It's full of strange, fascinating creatures. I'm telling you, these aliens, they're unlike anything we've seen before.

Yin: (studying the portal, unimpressed) They don't look that special, Yang. Miserable, kind of boring. Just another bunch of creatures stumbling through existence. What's so special about them?

Yang: (grinning mischievously) You're looking at the wrong ones. Trust me. There's one species one unlike any we've created before. I just... feel it. There's a portal to this realm, and I want us to explore it together.

Yin: (leaning back, sighing) I don't know... I created you because I needed company, and I've never once felt alone. I made the stars because you wanted something sparkly. You begged me to create these aliens, and now you want to leave our perfect world just to... what? Observe them up close? I don't see the appeal.

Yang: (softly, but excitedly) You don't have to see the appeal, Yin. Just come with me. It'll be a chance to experience something new. You're always so fixated on what we create on control. But I want to step beyond that. I want to feel something unexpected. Just a little bit of mystery.

Yin: (narrowing eyes) So, what? You want us to go on some random adventure just because you're bored? And if we get stuck there? We'll forget everything our home, our powers...

Yang: (grinning wider) Exactly. That's the fun part. We won't be our full selves. We won't remember everything, and that's what makes it exciting! Think about it we'll be in a place where we're not all powerful. Where we can be vulnerable. No safety net.

Yin: (folding arms, skeptical) And if I get into trouble? If some weird alien annoys me, I can't just zap them? What if they don't like the way I look?

Yang: (laughing softly) No, no zapping, Yin. But that's part of the beauty. We'll have each other. If anything goes wrong, we'll figure it out no powers, no memories, just us. Please, Yin. Let's see where this takes us.

(A long silence. Yin studies the swirling portal, uncertainty flickering in her expression. Yang watches eagerly, almost holding her breath.)

Yin: (exhaling deeply) Fine... But I'm not sure about this. I'm doing it for you, Yang. Just one last thing.

Yang: (smirking) You won't regret it. I promise.

Yin: (pointing) One last thing, Yang. You sure about this? We're not going to be able to zap anyone, right?

Yang: (laughing) Nope, no zapping! Just us and the unknown. Are you ready?

Yin: (smirking nervously) I guess so.

Yang: On three?

Yin: (taking a deep breath) One... Two... Three!

(Together, they leap into the portal, their figures dissolving into light. The cosmos ripples behind them as the world they created continues spinning, untouched, as they vanish into the unknown.)

Emma & Jeremiah Interlude

(Lights fade in, revealing a cozy yet modern therapist's office. A soft lamp casts a warm glow over the room. Ms. Chen sits calmly in her chair, a notepad in hand. Across from her, Emma and Jeremiah sit on a couch Emma, tense and frustrated, while Jeremiah looks concerned but composed.)

Emma: (leaning forward) Hello, Ms. Chen, my name is Emma, and this is my husband, Jeremiah. We're here today because my husband thinks I'm losing my mind.

Jeremiah: (quickly, shaking his head) Honey, I don't think you're losing your mind. I just think you're going through something... something you haven't fully figured out yet.

Emma: (annoyed) "Going through something"? That's what you think this is?

Ms. Chen: (softly, raising a hand) Alright, alright, let's take a step back. No need to rush, and let's avoid the name calling. We're here to listen and understand. Emma let's start with you. In your own words, tell me what's been happening.

Emma: (sighing, rubbing her temples) Okay, Ms. Chen. It all started about nine months ago. I began having these vivid visions... dreams... of two little girls. They're always the same these girls, their faces, their presence. It's like they're trying to tell me something, but I don't understand what.

Ms. Chen: (squinting slightly, curious) Hmm, I see. Are you two expecting a child?

Jeremiah: (quickly) No, we're not expecting.

Emma: (interjecting) I've already been checked out, Ms. Chen. Nothing physical is going on. But these dreams they feel so real, like they're trying to tell me something important.

Ms. Chen: (thoughtfully nodding) That's interesting. Dreams like that, especially if they're persistent, can sometimes point to something in your life. Do you two have a spiritual practice?

Emma: (shaking her head) No, not in the traditional sense. We're more spiritual than religious, I guess. I believe in energy, in the universe's pull. But big head here, he doesn't know what he believes half the time.

Jeremiah: (slightly defensive) I believe in the power within me, Emma. I don't need some conventional label to feel connected to the universe. But let's stay on topic here, please.

Emma: (sarcastically) Oh, now you want to stay on topic? Fine, go ahead.

Jeremiah: (frustrated but keeping his voice level) I'm not saying she's going crazy, Ms. Chen. I just don't know how to help her. These dreams... they've consumed her. She's so fixated on them that it's starting to wear on both of us.

Emma: (defensively) I'm sorry that I'm fixated on trying to understand what's happening to me, Jeremiah!

Jeremiah: (taking a deep breath, lowering his voice) That's not what I mean. It's just... I can't give you the answers, Emma. All I'm asking is that you take a moment to really dig deeper and look inside yourself for clarity. I can't help you find the answers you're looking for.

Ms. Chen: (gently interrupting) Emma, are you hearing what your husband is saying? It's clear that he's trying to be supportive. It sounds like he wants you to explore this on your own, but with patience.

Emma: (sighing, her frustration softening) I know. And I'm sorry for pushing him away. It's just... these dreams are so intense. I feel like they mean something bigger than just random visions. And I don't know why it's happening to me.

Jeremiah: (looking at her, his voice softer) I get it, Emma. I just... I'm not equipped to understand what's going on. And sometimes, it scares me because I don't want to see you hurting.

Ms. Chen: (with empathy) Emma, Jeremiah... It's clear that there's a strong bond between you two. The universe is showing you something, Emma, but it's up to you to be open to it. Take the time to quiet your mind, listen to your intuition, and trust in what comes up. It might not make sense right away, but you'll find clarity in time.

Emma: (nodding slowly, absorbing Ms. Chen's words) You're right. I've been so frantic about figuring it out that I haven't just listened. Maybe that's what I need to do.

Ms. Chen: (smiling) I'm glad you're open to it. Sometimes, the answers are already within us; we just have to stop trying so hard to find them. And Jeremiah be patient with her. She's working through something deep, something that takes time to process.

Jeremiah: (softly, reaching for Emma's hand) I will. I promise.

Ms. Chen: (breaking into a warm smile) Alright, because I like you two, I'm going to give you a discount today. But I do expect you to come back once you've figured it out, alright?

Emma & Jeremiah: (together, relieved) Thank you so much, Ms. Chen. We really appreciate everything.

Ms. Chen: (chuckling) No problem, my dear. Take care of each other, okay? And Emma remember to listen. The universe is trying to speak to you.

(Lights fade as the scene shifts to later that night.)

Later That Night

(Dim lighting. The bedroom is peaceful, the soft glow of the moon filtering through the curtains. Jeremiah stirs as Emma suddenly shakes him awake.)

Emma: (urgently) Jeremiah! Wake up!

Jeremiah: (groggy, rubbing his eyes) Baby, what's wrong? It's three in the morning...

Emma: (breathless, eyes wide) I know, but this is important. You have to listen to me.

Jeremiah: (sitting up, now worried) What is it? What's going on?

Emma: (whispering, almost reverent) It's about the girls... the ones in my dreams.

Jeremiah: (still confused, but more awake) You mean the girls you've been dreaming about?

Emma: (with growing certainty, her voice steady) Yes. They're coming, Jeremiah. They're real. They're going to need us.

(A slow fade to black as Jeremiah looks at Emma, his confusion deepening, while she stares ahead, as if seeing something he cannot.)

Chapter 1: The Twins Arrival

Emma reed was a dedicated teacher living in a middle-class neighborhood in Harlem. Her husband, Jeremiah reed, worked for a construction company, and together they led a quiet, content life.

One chilly morning, Emma was in the middle of teaching her class when a sharp pain gripped her stomach. She tried to push through the discomfort, but it became unbearable. Concerned, she excused herself and went straight to the hospital.

From the hospital bed, Emma called Jeremiah. I'm not feeling well, she said, her voice strained. I'm at the hospital.

Jeremiah's concern was evident. I'll leave work right now. Are you okay?

I don't know yet, Emma replied as a nurse entered the room.

Dr. Ross soon arrived, asking questions to narrow down the cause of Emma's pain. Do you think you ate something bad?

No, Emma said, shaking her head. All I had this morning was a bagel.

Is there a chance you could be pregnant? Dr. Ross asked.

Emma blinked, baffled. Pregnant? No, I don't think so.

The doctor nodded. Let's run some tests to find out what's going on.

Before the tests could even begin, Emma suddenly clutched her stomach and let out a cry of pain. It hurts so bad! she screamed.

Hearing Emma's distress over the phone, Jeremiah panicked. Emma? Baby, what's wrong?

Dr. Ross took the phone. Mr. Reed, your wife is in labor. We're taking her to the delivery room now.

Jeremiah was stunned. Labor? But we didn't even know

She'll be okay, Dr. Ross assured him. You need to get here as soon as possible.

Emma could hardly process what was happening as she was wheeled into the delivery room. I'm not pregnant! she insisted through the pain.

Dr. Ross looked at her calmly. Emma, I know this is a shock, but I need you to focus. On the count of three, I need you to push.

Still in disbelief, Emma did as instructed. With a final, powerful push, the room was filled with the first cries of a baby. A little girl with jet-black hair, shimmering like space and time itself, came into the world.

Emma barely had time to process the moment before Dr. Ross said, Wait I see another one. Emma, I need you to push again.

Summoning all her strength, Emma pushed one more time, and another baby girl emerged, this one with golden hair that seemed to glow like the sun.

The twins were placed in Emma's arms, and despite her exhaustion, she felt overwhelmed with love.

By the time Jeremiah arrived, tears were streaming down his face. Where's Emma? he asked the receptionist breathlessly.

Room 444, she replied.

Jeremiah sprinted to the room, bursting through the door to see his wife cradling two tiny bundles. Overcome with emotion, he kissed Emma's forehead and gazed at his newborn daughters.

Did you pick out names yet? he asked softly.

Emma nodded, a serene smile spreading across her face. Yes. Meet Yin and Yang.

Jeremiah looked at the twins one dark as night, the other radiant as the sun and knew the names were perfect. Yin and Yang, a harmonious balance of light and dark, had entered their lives and changed it forever.

When Yin and Yang turned three years old, Emma and Jeremiah enrolled them in pre-K. Their teacher, Ms. Allen, adored the twins but suggested they be placed in separate classes to help them develop their independence. After some thought, Emma and Jeremiah agreed, excited for the girls to start this new chapter. Yang was placed in the classroom directly across the hall from Yin's.

At first, the separation was difficult for the twins. Unfamiliar with their classmates, they would sit in their respective doorways during free time, playing with toys while keeping each other in sight. This became a daily habit, a quiet bond that neither of their teachers could ignore. Eventually, the teachers decided to close the classroom doors, believing this would encourage the girls to engage with their peers and make new friends.

Yang adapted quickly. Her sunny disposition drew other children to her, and she easily made friends. Yin, however, struggled. The kids in her class often teased her for sitting near the door, calling her a freak. Though their words hurt, Yin stayed near the doorway, hoping to catch a glimpse of her sister.

By the time the twins entered first grade, their differences had become even more pronounced. Yang was vibrant and social, while Yin grew more reserved and withdrawn. One day, as Yin stood by the classroom door like always, a boy named Jason approached her.

I like you. Do you want to play with me? he asked, smiling.

Yin's face lit up for the first time in ages. Yes, she replied softly.

The two went to the play area, drawing pictures, laughing, and being silly together. Their teacher, Ms. Carter, was relieved to see Yin finally engaging with someone. But not everyone was happy about this newfound friendship.

A girl named Tasha, who had a crush on Jason, was jealous of the attention he gave to Yin. She marched up to the pair and sneered, why are you playing with this freak?

Jason frowned. Because she's nice.

She's not nice! Tasha snapped. She just stands by the door like a weirdo, and her hair is ugly.

The cruel words struck a nerve in Yin. Anger surged through her, and before anyone could stop her, she punched Tasha in the face. Chaos erupted. Yin's rage spiraled out of control she began throwing toys and flipping chairs as tears streamed down her face.

The teachers scrambled to calm her down, but Yin was inconsolable. They had no choice but to call Emma and Jeremiah to the school immediately.

When the parents arrived, the classroom was a mess. Yin was screaming and thrashing, refusing to be comforted. Emma, desperate to help her daughter, had an idea. She asked the teachers to bring Yang to the classroom.

The moment Yang walked in; she ran to her sister's side. Gently, she took Yin's hand and hugged her tightly. That's enough, Yin, Yang whispered. It's okay now.

As if by magic, Yin's screaming stopped. Her breathing slowed, and she relaxed in her sister's arms. Jeremiah, watching the scene, noticed a faint glow surrounding the twins as they hugged.

Later, as the family drove home, Jeremiah couldn't stop thinking about what he'd seen. Did you notice the glow when they hugged? he asked Emma.

Emma shook her head. No, but I knew bringing Yang would help. Those two have always been so close I figured she could calm Yin down.

Jeremiah nodded. What do you think about putting them in the same class? That way, if Yin ever struggles again, Yang will be right there.

Emma hesitated, then agreed. You're right. It might help.

From that point on, Yin and Yang were placed in the same class. As Jeremiah predicted, Yang became Yin's anchor, always there to steady her when things got tough. Their bond only grew stronger as the years passed, and this pattern continued all the way to their senior year of high school.

Even though they were different as night and day, their connection was unshakable Yin's darkness and Yang's light balanced each other perfectly.

Emma and Jeremiah were thrilled as the day of the twins' prom and graduation approached. They spent weeks helping Yin and Yang prepare, taking them shopping for dresses, shoes, and accessories. Yang was excited she already had a prom date, her boyfriend Elijah, who had been her best friend since grade school. They were inseparable, sharing the same classes and friends.

Yin, on the other hand, didn't have a date. Though she was close to Yang, her standoffish nature kept her from forming relationships easily, especially with boys. Yang was worried about her sister. She wanted Yin to experience prom night fully, but Yin brushed off her concerns, saying, It's not a big deal. I'll be fine on my own.

One day, Elijah came up with an idea. My cousin Jason's back in town, he told Yang. He's our age and doesn't have a prom to go to. Maybe he could go with Yin?

Yang was skeptical. I don't know... Yin isn't big on blind setups.

Let me talk to him, Elijah insisted.

Meanwhile, at the mall, Yin was at the pretzel stand when she noticed a familiar face. She hesitated before tapping him on the shoulder. When he turned around, his face lit up.

Yin? Is that you?

Yin blinked. Jason?

He grinned. Wow, I haven't seen you since... first grade, right?

She nodded, laughing. Yeah, it's been a while. What are you doing back in town?

I'm visiting my cousin Elijah. Figured I'd take an early flight and surprise him.

They reminisced for a moment, laughing about the past especially the infamous day Yin punched Tasha. You had guts even back then, Jason said with a chuckle.

Yang and Elijah spotted them and walked over. Jason! Elijah shouted, clapping him on the back.

Jason laughed. What's up, cuz? I couldn't wait to get here.

Yang turned to Yin, surprised. You know him?

Yeah, we go way back, Yin said casually.

Elijah smirked. Perfect timing. We were just talking about you, Jason. Yin needs a prom date.

Jason's expression brightened. He turned to Yin. Would you go to prom with me?

Yin's cheeks flushed. You don't have to do that

I'm serious, Jason interrupted. I'd be honored to go with you.

After a moment of hesitation, Yin smiled. Well, in that case... I'd love to.

Jason grinned from ear to ear. Great! Let's make it a night to remember.

The twins spent the next few weeks hanging out with Jason and Elijah, preparing for prom. Jason even arranged to graduate alongside them, receiving special permission from his school to do so. Yin was thrilled, finally feeling a sense of belonging.

The night before prom, the group went to the roller-skating rink to celebrate. They were having a blast until Tasha and her crew showed up.

Yang noticed them first. Maybe we should go.

Jason shook his head. No way. We're here to have fun, and no one's ruining our night.

Yin agreed, determined not to let Tasha get under her skin. But when Jason went to the snack bar, Tasha made her move. She wrapped her arms around him and kissed him without warning.

Yin, who had been walking over to ask Jason for water, froze. Her chest tightened as she saw the kiss. Without saying a word, she turned and walked back to the dance floor.

Jason pushed Tasha away. What the hell are you doing?

Tasha smirked. I'm sorry, Jason. I couldn't help myself. She walked away, laughing, while Jason shook his head in frustration.

When he returned to the group, Yin was visibly upset. What's wrong? he asked, concerned.

Elijah cut in. Bro, tell me you weren't kissing Tasha.

Jason looked at Yin. It's not what it looked like. She kissed me

Why was she close enough to kiss you? Yin snapped, her voice trembling.

I don't know! I didn't see it coming.

Yin shook her head, hurt. I knew this was too good to be true.

Jason reached for her arm. Wait, don't do this. I'm here for you.

But Yin pulled away. I'm leaving. Yang let's go.

Yang hesitated but followed her sister.

When they got home, Yin sat on the edge of her bed, tears streaming down her face. Why does this always happen to me, Yang? No one ever treats me like I matter. People like you more. They always have.

Yang knelt beside her. What are you talking about? We're identical. We're the same.

No, we're not. You're beautiful, with your golden hair and light. Everyone notices you. No one notices me.

Yang's heart ached for her sister. Yin, your hair is beautiful. It's like the universe mysterious, endless, and full of wonder. Sometimes I wish mine were like yours.

Yin sniffled, a small smile forming. You really mean that?

Of course I do, Yang said. And for what it's worth, Jason cares about you. You need to let him explain.

Yin sighed. Maybe... I'll think about it.

Yang hugged her tightly. I love you, sis. Don't let anyone make you feel less than what you are.

I love you too, Yin whispered.

The night ended on a note of sisterly love, as it always did when the twins leaned on each other.

Yin woke up to her phone ringing incessantly. Groaning, she grabbed it off the nightstand and answered without checking the caller ID.

What? she snapped.

Jason's voice came through, calm but slightly exasperated. Well, damn. Good morning to you too.

Yin rolled her eyes. Jason, why are you blowing up my phone? What do you want?

I'm trying to explain what happened last night.

There's nothing to explain. You like dusty girls. Case closed. Look, I can't deal with this right now. Goodbye.

Wait! Jason said quickly. What about tonight? The limo? Prom?

What about it? she asked coldly.

Elijah and I already booked the limo. We're still picking you and Yang up.

That's fine, Yin said flatly. But don't come in my house, and don't speak to me in the limo either. Without giving him a chance to respond, she hung up.

Yang, who had been half listening from across the room, shook her head. You're being stubborn.

Yin sighed, tossing her phone onto the bed. I don't care. How did he let Tasha get that close to him? It's basic common sense.

Yang smirked. You know these guys are clueless. He probably wasn't paying attention. But listen Jason likes you. A guy who's playing games wouldn't be going this hard to fix things.

Yin leaned back, crossing her arms. Maybe you're right... but I'm not making it easy for him. He's going to have to prove it.

Yang grinned. Fair enough. Now let's get ready we've got hair and nail appointments to make!

The Morning Rush

When the girls came downstairs, the delicious smell of breakfast filled the house. Emma and Jeremiah had prepared a feast: pancakes, eggs, bacon, fresh fruit, and more.

Good morning, my beautiful graduates! Emma said, beaming with pride.

Jeremiah clapped his hands. Come on, dig in! Big day ahead!

Yin and Yang wasted no time, piling their plates high and eating quickly.

Whoa, slow down, Jeremiah chuckled. What's the rush?

Emma laughed. They've got appointments, remember? Hair, nails, the whole nine yards.

Jeremiah nodded, pretending to sigh. Ah, I see. My girls are too grown to hang out with their dad all morning.

Yang giggled. Daddy, you know we need a ride.

Jeremiah grinned. Say no more. Let's get moving.
The twins hugged their mom goodbye, thanking her for breakfast, and followed their dad out to the car.

The salon buzzed with energy as Yin and Yang walked in. Women of all ages were chatting, laughing, and showing off pictures of their dream styles. Yin glanced around, feeling a bit more at ease.

What are you girls getting today? Juanita the stylist asked with a warm smile.

Something magical, Yang said confidently, flipping her golden hair.

Yin smirked. Just make us look good.

As Juanita the stylists got back to work on Yang's hair, Yin's mind wandered. She couldn't stop thinking about Jason's persistence. Was Yang, right? Could he really be telling the truth?

Yang nudged her. You're quiet. What's on your mind?

Nothing, Yin muttered.

Yang raised an eyebrow. Liar.

Yin sighed. I'm just... thinking about tonight. What if I made a mistake?

Yang smiled. If he's the guy you think he is, he'll prove it. Just give him a chance, sis.

Yin nodded, deciding she'd let the night play out. After all, prom was supposed to be magical, and she wasn't about to let anyone ruin it not Tasha, not Jason, and certainly not her own doubts.

As Yin and Yang sat in the salon getting their hair done, Yang noticed someone walk in. She leaned toward her sister, whispering, don't look now, but guess who just showed up?

Yin glanced up, and her eyes narrowed when she saw Tasha Walk in with her usual smug look.

Before Yin could react, Juanita, the stylist, walked over to her. Ashley's running a bit late. If you don't mind, I can do your hair or do want to wait, she offered kindly.

Yin hesitated but nodded. Sure, I'll wait, since you still need to do Yang's hair anyway.

Juanita smiled and went to work. But across the room, Tasha couldn't help herself. She saw the twins and decided to make her presence known. I guess Ashley's running late because she doesn't want to do your ugly ass hair, she sneered.

Yang instantly spun around, her temper flaring. Chill the hell out, Tasha. What's your problem?

Tasha scoffed. Your sister is my problem. She gets on my damn nerves.

Yin, who had been calm up until now, stood up, her voice cool but cutting. How exactly do I get on your nerves? You're just jealous.

Jealous of what? Tasha spat, stepping closer.

Jealous because I'm with Jason, and you're not, Yin shot back.

Tasha smirked. Oh, you're still with him? I guess it didn't work, huh?

Yang stepped forward, standing protectively in front of Yin. What didn't work? You kissing Jason? Yeah, we know what really happened.

Tasha scoffed. Oh, he told you.

Yin crossed her arms, staring Tasha down. Don't try to pretend you didn't see me coming toward you so you could pretend he kissed you to get me jealous. But guess what? I'm not jealous of a dusty bitch.

Tasha's anger flared, and she lunged at Yin, but Yang was faster. She leaped into the space between them, hands raised. Don't you dare touch my sister.

Juanita had heard enough and called out, Tasha, you need to leave. Now.

Tasha glared at Yin but knew better than to argue with Juanita. I'm not done with you, she hissed before storming out of the salon.

Later that night, the twins were getting ready for prom, each of them radiant and glowing. Meanwhile, Jason and Elijah were nervously preparing themselves. Jason's mind was a whirlwind of thoughts he knew Yin was upset with him, and he wasn't sure if he should go all in with a bold approach or honor her request and stay in the limo.

Elijah, sensing Jason's nerves, clapped him on the back. Man, I think you should go in. That's your future right there.

Jason chuckled nervously. Yeah, with a little more confidence, maybe.

Elijah laughed. She's got you sprung, huh?

Jason grinned. And Yang's got you wide open, cuz, so let's not talk about it.

Elijah smirked but didn't argue. Moments later, Elijah's mom walked in, smiling at the sight of the two boys looking so grown up. Look at you two! The limo's here, are you ready?

Yeah, Mom. We're ready, Elijah said with a wink. His mom took several pictures, much to the boys' dismay.

After the pictures were done, they headed to the limo, both boys buzzing with anticipation. The twins, meanwhile, had decided to switch dresses for the night. Yang wore the black dress, and Yin wore the gold one. When they came downstairs, Emma's eyes welled up with tears.

Look at our babies, Emma said softly. They're all grown up.

Jeremiah was trying to keep it together, snapping pictures. Honey, you're going to make me cry too.

The doorbell rang just as they were preparing to leave. Emma smiled, wiping away a tear, and opened the door to reveal the boys standing there, looking sharp.

Elijah walked in first, a proud smile on his face. Jason hesitated, his gaze meeting Yin's. Come on in, Yin said, smiling warmly. You look handsome tonight.

Jason couldn't help but beam, his nerves melting away. As he stepped inside, the boys exchanged corsages Jason giving Elijah the black one, and Elijah giving Jason the gold one. They each kissed the twins on the cheek, and Jeremiah snapped several more pictures before they made their way to the limo.

Once inside, Jason turned to Yin, still unsure. So... does this mean you forgive me?

Yin smiled softly. You don't have to apologize. You told me the truth, and I just needed to hear it for myself. I believe you.

Jason exhaled in relief. So how did you know?

Yin turned toward him, a faint smile on her lips. The universe revealed it to me.

Elijah popped open the champagne, and the limo filled with laughter and music as they headed to prom.

When the group entered the prom, all eyes were on the twins. They were stunning, and the room seemed to stop for a moment as they made their entrance. Compliments flooded in from every direction. Jason and Elijah stood proudly by their sides, feeling lucky to be with two of the most beautiful girls in the room.

The night was magical dancing, singing, and enjoying the music as the DJ played songs from Harlem's legendary artists. But as the night went on, the announcement for prom king and queen came.

Dean Perry took the stage, calling for everyone's attention. The tension in the room was palpable as the nominees stood by, fingers crossed. When Jason's name was called for prom king, he stood, shocked. How? I don't even go here, he said, but Elijah laughed. Don't worry, bro. This one's on me.

Jason walked to the stage, still stunned, and was crowned prom king. Then Dean Perry called out Yin's name for prom queen. Yin, equally shocked, looked at Yang. I didn't even run for it, she said, confused.

Yang smiled, her eyes sparkling. I nominated you. You deserve it, sis.

Yin felt a surge of pride as she walked to the stage, Jason waiting for her. They shared a dance as the crowd cheered. But suddenly, the sprinklers went off, drenching everyone in water.

As Yin looked up, she saw Tasha standing with a red cup, smirking. Before Yin could react, Tasha splashed her dress with red paint. That's what you get, bitch! she shouted.

Yang saw the fire ignite in Yin's eyes. She reached for her hand, but Yin slapped her hand away. Not this time, Yin muttered, her voice icy with rage. She could barely control herself. The years of torment, the bullying, everything Tasha had done to her came rushing to the surface. Her eyes turned black, and the ground beneath them began to shake.

Tasha's friends tried to intervene, but they were no match for the energy radiating from Yin. She grabbed Tasha by the throat, lifting her off the ground. The gym around them began to crumble, and flames erupted from the walls.

Yang shouted for Yin to calm down, but her sister was too far gone. Yin, please, Yang cried.

Jason, desperate to stop her, ran to Yin. I know what it's like. I know what people say behind your back. But you can't let them win. You're beautiful. You've always been beautiful.

Yin's gaze softened for a moment, and Yang stepped closer. You are beautiful. Don't let this rage define you.

Jeremiah's voice broke through. Yin, grab her hand, honey!

Yang reached out and took Yin's hand. I need you, Yin.

With tears streaming down her face, Yin finally grabbed her sister's hand. As they embraced, a powerful light enveloped them. The fire ceased, and the building began to repair itself, brick by brick.

And then, as quickly as it had all begun, the twins disappeared.

After Prom

In the months that followed the prom night, Emma and Jeremiah couldn't quite comprehend the events that transpired. They searched for answers, but nothing made sense. The twins were gone. Jason and Elijah were left in devastation, unable to explain the inexplicable disappearance of the girls. No one knew where they had gone, why it had happened, or how to process it.

For weeks, the house was quiet too quiet. The absence of Yin and Yang left a void that no one could fill.

Finally, after what seemed like an eternity, Tasha awoke from her coma. Her parents were relieved to see their daughter alive, but Tasha was consumed by one thought: Yin. As soon as she regained consciousness, her first words we're I need to apologize to Yin.

Tasha, sweetheart, there's something you need to know, her mother began gently. On the night of prom... Yin and Yang disappeared.

Tasha blinked in confusion. What do you mean, they disappeared?

Her father, unsure how to explain the unexplainable, sighed deeply. I don't know, honey. They're just gone. It's like they never existed.

The words hung in the air, heavy with unanswered questions, and Tasha could only stare in disbelief. She had no idea what had happened that night, and she couldn't grasp how it was even possible for the twins to be gone.

The Unexpected Return

Months passed. The seasons changed, and life in the house began to resume some normalcy, though Emma couldn't shake the feeling of something missing. One morning, she decided to finally clean up the twins' room. It had been nine months since she'd stepped foot in there too long.

As she entered the room, a strange feeling washed over her. The beds were exactly as they had been the night the girls disappeared. But as she got closer to the beds, something unusual caught her eye. She squinted, then froze. There, lying in the exact same positions they had always slept in, were the twins.

Jeremiah! Emma gasped, her voice shaking with disbelief.

Jeremiah rushed into the room, eyes wide. What is it, honey?

When he saw them, he couldn't believe his own eyes. His daughters alive and breathing were asleep in their beds as if no time had passed at all.

Girls, he called, his voice thick with emotion.

Yin and Yang stirred, blinking their eyes open and stretching as if they'd just woken from a long nap. Yes, Dad? they said in unison.

Emma broke down in tears, her emotions overwhelming her. Where have you girls been? We've been searching for you... we thought we lost you forever.

Yin and Yang exchanged a brief, knowing look before Yin replied softly, we've been home.

Jeremiah stood in stunned silence, his heart racing. Home? What do you mean, home?

But the girls didn't elaborate. They were back, and that was all that mattered.

Later that day, the twins, still in a daze from everything that had happened, decided to go see Jason and Elijah. The boys had been worried sick, unsure of what had happened to the twins, and they had spent months trying to find answers. The reunion was nothing short of surreal.

When the twins walked into Elijah's house, Jason and Elijah were speechless. Jason's eyes went wide as he stared at them, his mouth slightly open.

Where have you guys been? Jason asked, disbelief still coloring his voice.

Yin smiled softly and shook her head. Don't think too hard about it, or your brain might hurt, she teased, though she couldn't hide the fatigue in her eyes.

Yang glanced around, suddenly aware of how hungry she felt. I'm starving. Feels like I haven't eaten in months, she admitted with a grin.

Yin laughed and nodded. Same here. Are you guys hungry too?

Jason and Elijah exchanged glances, relieved and amused. You bet we are, Elijah replied. Let's go grab some pizza.

At the pizza shop, the twins, Jason, and Elijah made their way to a table, eager to enjoy a relaxing meal after everything that had happened. But as they approached the counter, they noticed a familiar face Tasha, accompanied by her friends.

Tasha's eyes immediately locked onto Yin. She hesitated for a moment before walking up to her. Yin tensed, but before Tasha could get any closer, Jason stepped in front of her.

Tasha, what are you doing? Jason asked, his voice firm but calm.

Tasha, with a mix of guilt and sincerity, sighed. I'm not here to start anything, Jason. I... I owe Yin an apology.

Yin studied her for a moment, unsure of how to react. Tasha had caused so much pain, and yet Yin could feel something different in her energy now. Tasha wasn't the same person she had been before, but yin didn't care.

Yin took a deep breath. You're not forgiven.
The words slipped from Yin's lips, cold and cutting, carrying a venom that left the air thick with tension. Tasha stood frozen, disbelief flickering in her eyes who did

Yin think she was. The audacity, the sheer arrogance of it, made her chest tighten, but for a moment, she couldn't even find the words to respond.

With the tension still high between them, the girls took their trays of pizza and made their way to their table, leaving Tasha standing there.

Jason watched Yin, still amazed at her strength. You're amazing, you know that? he said softly, his voice full of admiration.

Yin smiled at him, her heart full. I love you, she whispered.

Jason grinned back. I love you too.

And for the first time in a long time, everything felt right again.

Chapter 2: Shadows of the Past

Even though Yin and Yang were back, nothing felt the same. Their parents, Emma and Jeremiah, did their best to pretend life had returned to normal, but the twins' absence had left a void that couldn't simply be filled overnight.

Emma noticed how quiet Yin had become, often staring out of the window or spending hours in the backyard under the stars. Yang, on the other hand, threw herself into a whirlwind of energy, laughing louder and staying out longer than usual, as if trying to compensate for her sister's silence.

One night, as the family sat down for dinner, Jeremiah finally broke the tension.

I think it's time we talked about what happened, he said, looking at the twins.

Yin's fork clattered against her plate. Yang glanced at her sister, her usual confident expression faltering.

We already told you, Yang said quickly. We were home the whole time.

Emma's voice trembled. But you weren't. Not really. Your beds were empty for nine months. The entire town thought... She paused, taking a shaky breath. We thought we lost you.

Yin pushed her chair back and stood abruptly. We don't have to do this right now.

Yin Jeremiah started, but she was already walking out of the room.

Yang sighed. Give her time, Dad. She's still figuring things out.

And you're not? Emma asked, her eyes searching Yang's face.

Yang hesitated. We're fine, Mom. Really.

But as the twins left the table, Emma and Jeremiah exchanged worried glances. Something wasn't right.

Across Town

Jason and Elijah were sitting in Elijah's basement, playing video games, but neither of them could focus. The return of the twins weighed heavily on their minds.

You notice how Yin's... different? Jason asked, setting down his controller.

Elijah nodded. Yeah. Yang too. Like, they're trying too hard to act normal.

Jason sighed. It's like they're hiding something. And I can't shake what we saw at prom how everything went up in flames, and then they just vanished.

Elijah leaned back, crossing his arms. What are you going to do?

I don't know, Jason admitted. But I need to talk to Yin. I can't just pretend nothing happened.

That night, Yin sat by the river, her usual escape, but something about the water felt off. The moon's reflection rippled unnaturally, the light twisting and bending as if it were alive.

Still hiding, huh? Yang's voice broke through the silence as she joined her sister on the riverbank.

I'm not hiding, Yin replied without looking up.

Yang smirked. Sure, you're not.

For a moment, neither of them spoke. Then Yang sighed. You feel it too, don't you? Like we're different now.

Yin finally turned to her sister; her dark eyes filled with unease. What happened to us, Yang? Where did we go? I can't remember anything, but I know we weren't... here.

Yang nodded slowly. I don't know either. But whatever it was, it changed us. You saw what you did at prom. That wasn't just anger, Yin. It was... something else."

Yin hugged her knees to her chest, her voice barely a whisper. What if it happens again?
Yang placed a reassuring hand on her shoulder. Then we face it Together like we always do.

But as the twins stared out at the river, they couldn't shake the feeling that their return was only the beginning, and the shadows of the past were still chasing them.

Chapter 3: Echoes of Another World

The unease surrounding the twins' return only deepened in the weeks that followed. Yin and Yang began noticing strange occurrences small at first but increasingly difficult to ignore.

It started with mirrors.

Yin stood in the bathroom one evening, brushing her hair, when the reflection behind her flickered. For a moment, the image in the mirror wasn't her it was a darker version, her eyes black and empty, her lips twisted in a sinister smile.

She dropped the brush with a gasp, spinning around. The bathroom was empty.

Yang? she called out, her voice trembling.

Yang appeared in the doorway moments later, concern etched on her face. What's wrong?

Yin pointed to the mirror. I... I saw something. It wasn't me.

Yang glanced at the mirror, her expression hardening. We're not alone anymore, are we?

One night, as the twins searched the attic for old photo albums, they stumbled across something neither of them remembered: a locked door.

Since when has this been here? Yang asked, running her fingers over the smooth, untouched wood.

Yin shook her head. I don't know. I've never seen it before.

They called for Jeremiah, who climbed up to inspect it. That's impossible, he muttered. I built this house myself. There's no way a door just appears out of nowhere.

Emma joined them, her face pale. Jeremiah, she whispered, pointing to the frame. That symbol...

Carved into the wood was an intricate sigil that seemed to glow faintly in the dim light.

I've seen this before, Emma said, her voice shaky.

When? Yin asked, stepping closer.

In my grandmother's journals. She always warned about... places that connect to other realms. She said these symbols were gateways.

Yang's eyes widened. Gateways? To what?

Emma swallowed hard. I don't know. But if this is here, then something's trying to come through.

That night, Yin dreamed.

She was standing in an endless field of darkness, stars blinking faintly above her. A voice echoed all around a voice that sounded like her own but deeper, colder.

You don't remember, do you? the voice said.

Remember what? Yin called out.

The shadows shifted, forming into a figure. It was her dark reflection from the mirror.

You were chosen, the shadow said, stepping closer. You and your sister. You've been given a gift.

What gift? Yin asked, her voice trembling.

The shadow smirked. You'll find out soon enough.

When Yin woke up, her heart was racing. She rushed to Yang's room, only to find her sister sitting on the floor, surrounded by glowing sigils that floated in the air.

Yang, what are you doing?

Yang looked up, her eyes glowing faintly. I don't know. I woke up, and this just... started happening.

Yin stepped closer, but the sigils flared brighter, pushing her back.

It's connected to the door, Yang said, her voice oddly calm. Whatever's on the other side, it's calling to us.

Yin clenched her fists. Then we need to stop it.

Yang shook her head. You don't understand, Yin. I think we're part of it. This power it's not just something we have. It's something we are.

The twins decided to confront the door. With their parents too frightened to intervene, it was up to them to discover the truth.

As they approached, the sigil on the door glowed brighter, and a low hum filled the air. Yin hesitated.

What if we can't handle what's on the other side? she asked.

Yang placed a hand on her shoulder. We'll handle it. Together.

With a deep breath, they pushed the door open.

Beyond the threshold was not the attic but an entirely different world a realm of shifting shadows and glowing lights, filled with echoes of laughter and whispers of fear.

And in the center of it all stood a figure cloaked in darkness, waiting for them.

Chapter 4: The Shadowed Figure

The figure cloaked in darkness radiated an energy that made the air vibrate. As Yin and Yang stepped cautiously into the shifting realm, the being tilted its head, as if studying them.

You've finally arrived, it said, its voice layered with countless echoes, male and female, old and young.

Who are you? Yin demanded, her voice firm despite the fear clawing at her chest.

The figure stepped closer, the shadows peeling back slightly to reveal a face that mirrored both of theirs a strange fusion of Yin and Yang, with eyes that shifted between gold and black.

I am the origin, it said. I am the balance between light and darkness. And I am the one who chose you.

Yang's eyes narrowed. Chose us for what?

The figure's gaze pierced through them, and for a moment, the world around them shimmered with images of stars being born and galaxies collapsing.

You were not born merely as human beings, it said. You are embodiments of cosmic forces opposite but intertwined. Light and shadow. Chaos and order. Together, you maintain balance. But apart...

The figure's eyes darkened, and the realm seemed to tremble. Apart, you risk unraveling everything.

The figure extended a hand, and the twins were suddenly overwhelmed with memories not of their human lives, but of something far older.
They saw themselves as glowing entities in a void, weaving stars and creating worlds. They saw their bond, an eternal thread connecting them, guiding them as they worked in harmony.

But then the vision darkened. They saw conflict Yang consumed by chaos; Yin overwhelmed by despair. The thread that bound them began to fray, and the worlds they created began to crumble.

Do you see now? the figure asked. You are creators, but also destroyers. Your bond is the foundation of all you touch. If it breaks, so does everything else.

Yin stepped forward, her voice trembling with a mix of awe and anger. If we're so important, why don't we remember any of this?

The figure's expression softened. You were given human lives to learn humility, to understand the value of what you create. But the time has come to awaken your true selves.

Yang crossed her arms. And what if we don't want this? What if we just want to live normal lives?

The figure's eyes flickered with sadness. That choice was made long ago, when you first chose to exist as one. You cannot escape what you are. But you can choose how to use it.

Before the twins could respond, the realm around them began to quake. The figure turned sharply, its form shifting into a defensive stance.

They've found us, it muttered.

Who? Yin asked, her voice rising with fear.

The Wreckers, the figure said. Entities that feed on imbalance. They've been following your chaos, sensing your instability. They will destroy this realm and your world if they are not stopped.

Yang clenched her fists. Then tell us what to do.

The figure faced them again, its gaze fierce. Your bond is the key. You must align your powers light and shadow in harmony. Only then can you repel the Wreckers. As the shadows around them thickened, figures began to emerge monstrous, shifting shapes that seemed to devour the light. The Wreckers advanced, their movements chaotic and relentless.

Yin and Yang instinctively moved closer to each other.

I don't know if I can do this, Yin admitted, her voice shaking.

Yang grabbed her hand. You're not doing this alone. We're in this together, like always.

The figure nodded approvingly. Focus on your bond. Let it guide you.

Closing their eyes, the twins began to feel the connection between them a thread of energy that pulsed with life. Yin's calm steadied Yang's chaos, while Yang's fire reignited Yin's hope.

As the thread glowed brighter, the twins began to transform. Yin's form radiated with golden light, while Yang became a swirling vortex of shadow. Together, they were a dazzling force of balance.

A Battle for Balance

The Wreckers lunged, but the twins fought back, their powers weaving together in perfect harmony. Each blast of energy they unleashed restored parts of the realm, driving the Wreckers further back.

The figure watched, its expression unreadable. This is only the beginning, it murmured.

As the last Wrecker dissolved into nothingness, the realm stabilized, its chaotic shifts calming into a serene, star filled expanse.

Yin and Yang turned to the figure, their forms still glowing with power.

What now? Yang asked.

The figure smiled faintly. You have proven that you can unite, even under pressure. But maintaining balance is a lifelong journey. Your world and many others depend on you.

Chapter 5: The Return to Earth

The twins awoke in their beds, disoriented but aware of everything that had transpired. The air in their room was thick with an unfamiliar energy, and the bond between them hummed like a steady pulse in their chests.

Yin rubbed her temples, still processing the battle and the revelations about their true nature. Was it all real? she asked Yang, who sat cross-legged on the bed, staring at her glowing hands.

It felt real, Yang replied, flexing her fingers. The faint shimmer of shadow energy flickered and then receded. And I don't think we're the same anymore.

Before they could say more, Emma and Jeremiah burst into the room, their faces a mixture of relief and fear.

You're back, Emma cried, rushing to embrace them. You've been gone for so long. Where were you?

Yin hesitated, exchanging a glance with Yang. It's... a long story, she said.

Later that day, Yin and Yang visited Jason and Elijah. The boys were stunned to see them and bombarded them with questions about where they had been.

We were in... another place, Yin said carefully, trying to explain without revealing too much.

Yang jumped in. Look, it's complicated. But the important thing is we're back now.

Jason wasn't convinced. He looked directly at Yin, his concern evident. You disappeared for months. And now you're acting like everything's fine. What's really going on?

Yin hesitated, the weight of the truth pressing against her. She felt the bond with Yang tighten, as if urging her to trust Jason.

We're different, she admitted. Something happened to us, and we're trying to figure it out.

Jason softened, reaching out to take her hand. You don't have to figure it out alone.

As days turned into weeks, the twins found themselves grappling with their new abilities.

Yin struggled to control the light that seemed to pour out of her in moments of heightened emotion. Once, while arguing with Jason, her frustration caused a burst of energy that shattered a lamp.

Yang's powers were equally unpredictable. Her shadow energy often responded to her impulsive nature, creating flickers of darkness that startled anyone nearby.

Elijah, ever the optimist, tried to keep things light. So, what are you guys? Superheroes now?

Yang smirked. Something like that.

But Yin shook her head. This isn't a game. If we mess up, we could hurt people or worse.

One afternoon, while the twins were walking through town, they encountered Tasha. She looked nervous but determined as she approached them.

I... I just wanted to say thank you, Tasha said, her voice unsteady. For saving me.

Yang raised an eyebrow. Saving you? We weren't exactly thinking about you that night.

Tasha shook her head. You don't get it. After what happened at prom, I started seeing things, shadows, lights, things I couldn't explain. It's like... you left a part of yourselves behind.

Yin and Yang exchanged a worried glance.

That night, the twins sat together in their room, the weight of their new reality sinking in.

We can't go back to the way things were, Yin said quietly.

Yang sighed, leaning back against the headboard. I know. But what does that mean for us? For Jason and Elijah? For Mom and Dad?

Yin looked out the window at the stars. It means we must find a way to balance this life and the one we left behind. If we don't...

Yang finished her thought, everything falls apart.

Chapter 6: Balancing Worlds

The twins soon realized that balancing their old lives with their new responsibilities was far more complicated than they had imagined. Their powers seemed to bleed into their daily routines, and the effects on those around them were becoming impossible to ignore.

Yin started noticing how her emotions were directly influencing her powers. One evening, during a study session with Jason, she became frustrated over a calculus problem. Her hands lit up, sending a surge of radiant energy through the room and short circuiting the lamp.

Yin! Jason exclaimed, jumping back.

I'm sorry! she said, holding her glowing hands to her chest. I didn't mean to.

Jason moved closer; his worry etched on his face. You've got to get this under control. What happens if it's not a lamp next time?

Yin nodded, but the weight of it all was suffocating. I'm trying, Jason. I am.

Yang, on the other hand, found her powers seeping into her dreams. At night, the shadows in her room would twist and dance, forming shapes that whispered to her in an unfamiliar language. She confided in Elijah, who tried to reassure her.

Maybe it's your subconscious, Elijah said one night while they sat in his car. Your powers are trying to tell you something.

Yang shrugged. Or maybe I'm losing my mind.

Elijah took her hand. You're not. You're stronger than you think.

Meanwhile, Tasha's strange experiences were growing more intense. She started seeing flashes of light and shadow in her peripheral vision, and sometimes she would hear whispers that sounded eerily like Yin and Yang's voices.

One day, she confronted the twins outside of school.

You need to tell me what's happening to me, Tasha demanded, her eyes wild. I keep seeing things hearing things. It's like your powers left a mark on me.

Yin frowned. What do you mean?

Tasha hesitated. Ever since prom, it's like... I can feel your presence, even when you're not around. And when I get angry, weird things happen.

Yang crossed her arms. Like what?

Tasha looked away, embarrassed. Like the other day, I broke a mirror just by looking at it. And I wasn't even touching it!

Yin and Yang exchanged a concerned glance.

This isn't normal, Yin said. You shouldn't have powers. We need to figure out why this is happening.

The twins decided to return to the mysterious realm where they had first unlocked their powers. Using the connection they now shared, they concentrated and willed themselves back to the glowing field of stars.

The mysterious figure was waiting for them.

You've returned, the figure said, their voice echoing. Good. There is much to discuss.

Why is this happening to Tasha? Yin demanded.

And why are our powers so unstable? Yang added.

The figure's form shimmered as they spoke. "Your powers are not merely abilities they are extensions of the universe itself. When you act with strong emotion, you leave imprints on the world around you. Tasha is one such imprint.

Yang frowned. So, we did this to her?

The figure nodded. Unintentionally, yes. But she is now tethered to your energy. If left unchecked, this connection could destabilize her and you."

Yin felt a pang of guilt. How do we fix it?

You must teach her to balance the energy within her, the figure said. Just as you must learn to balance your own.

Teaching Tasha

Back on Earth, the twins reluctantly approached Tasha with the truth. At first, Tasha was resistant, still harboring bitterness over Yin not accepting her apology.

You want to help me? Tasha scoffed. Why? So, you can feel better about yourselves?

No, Yang said firmly. We want to help because if we don't, you'll lose control. And it's not just you who will suffer everyone around you will, too.

Tasha hesitated, then nodded. Fine. But don't think this makes us friends. Yin sneered at Tasha, you don't have to worry about that, I'm only helping you because if I don't innocent people will get hurt.

The twins began teaching her to control the fragments of power she had absorbed. It was a difficult process, fraught with tension and setbacks. But slowly, Tasha began to stabilize.

As the twins spent more time helping Tasha, their relationships with Jason and Elijah began to strain.

Jason felt left out, his concern for Yin turning into frustration. Why do you keep pushing me away? he asked her one night.

I'm not trying to, Yin said, her voice cracking. I'm just... dealing with things you can't understand.

Then help me understand, Jason pleaded.

Yang's bond with Elijah was similarly tested. The usually lighthearted Elijah grew increasingly serious as he noticed Yang pulling away.

You don't have to do this alone, he told her.

Yang shook her head. But I do. If I mess up, people could get hurt. I won't risk that.
One night, while meditating to strengthen their bond, Yin and Yang had a shared vision. They saw Earth cracking, its balance disrupted by a growing fissure between light and shadow.

The figure from the mysterious realm appeared in the vision.

This is the future you must prevent, the figure said. Your powers are tied to the balance of the universe. If you do not reconcile your duality light and shadow the Earth will fall.

When the vision ended, the twins looked at each other, their determination renewed.

We must fix this, Yin said.

Yang nodded. Together.

Chapter 7: Restoring the Balance

The twins, now aware of the weight of their responsibilities, began to prepare for their journey to prevent the catastrophic future they had seen. The vision haunted them Earth cracking under the strain of their imbalance, the fissure between light and shadow threatening to consume everything.

They decided to return to the mysterious realm to seek guidance from the figure who had been their guide.

Back in the glowing field of stars, the figure stood waiting. This time, their form seemed more defined less of a blur, more human like, though still ethereal.

You understand the stakes now, the figure said. The balance of Earth depends on your unity.

We get that, Yang said. But how do we stop this from happening?

The figure gestured, and a swirling orb of light appeared before them, showing fragments of the Earth's energy grid. Your world is held together by points of equilibrium nodes where light and shadow meet. Some of these have grown unstable due to your imbalance.

Yin squinted at the orb. So, we need to stabilize them?

Yes, the figure confirmed. But it is not merely about repairing the nodes. It is about understanding yourselves your connection to one another and to this duality. Only through harmony can the balance be restored.

The First Node

Their journey took them to the first node, a remote forest in the Pacific Northwest. The air felt charged with energy as they approached the heart of the forest, where a massive, ancient tree stood. Its roots stretched deep into the Earth, glowing faintly with light and shadow.

Is this it? Yang asked.

Yin nodded. It must be.

As they stepped closer, the ground began to tremble. Shadows erupted from the Earth, twisting into monstrous forms that roared and lunged at them.

Yang's hands ignited with darkness, and Yin's with light. Together, they fought back, their powers weaving in harmony. But the creatures seemed endless, feeding off their frustration and fear.

We're not winning, Yang shouted, blocking an attack.

Yin paused, her light flickering. Maybe that's the problem. We're fighting.

What do you mean?

Look at them, Yin said, pointing at the creatures. They're just extensions of us our imbalance.

Yang hesitated, then nodded. Okay. So, what do we do?

Stop resisting, Yin said, lowering her hands.

Yang followed suit, and as they stood still, the creatures hesitated. Slowly, Yin and Yang reached out their hands, touching the shadows. The creatures dissolved, merging back into the Earth.

The glowing tree stabilized, its light and shadow intertwining perfectly.

Their victory at the first node came with a revelation they needed to trust not only each other but themselves.

Later that night, as they rested near the forest, Yang broke the silence.

You were right back there, she said. About the creatures. I was so ready to fight, I didn't think about what they really were.

We both have our instincts, Yin replied. Yours is to defend, mine is to heal. We just need to learn when to use them.

Yang smirked. Look at us, growing and stuff.

Yin laughed. Don't get used to it.

Meanwhile, back on Earth, Tasha began noticing strange disruptions around her. Lights flickered when she walked into rooms, and small objects would levitate when she was angry or upset.

She confronted Jason and Elijah, who had been trying to piece together what the twins were doing.

They're fixing the balance, aren't they? Tasha asked.

Jason nodded. That's what it sounds like.

Then why is this still happening to me? Tasha demanded, gesturing at a floating pen.

Elijah frowned. Maybe it's because you're still connected to them. If they don't fix everything, it could get worse.

Tasha crossed her arms. Then we need to find them and make sure they finish the job

The Second Node

The second node lay deep within an abandoned city, where light barely penetrated the heavy shadows. As the twins approached, they felt the pull of the imbalance growing stronger.

This time, the test was different. Instead of external creatures, the shadows and light twisted into mirrors of themselves.

Yang stared at her dark reflection, which smirked at her. You think you're so strong, don't you? it said. But you're just scared of being vulnerable.

Yin faced her glowing double, which shook its head. You hide behind kindness, afraid to show your true power.

The twins glanced at each other, unsure how to proceed.

What now? Yang whispered.

Maybe... Yin hesitated. Maybe we listen to them.

Yang raised an eyebrow. Listen to our evil twins?

They're not evil, Yin said. They're us. Parts of us we need to face.

Taking a deep breath, they turned to their reflections, ready to confront the truths they had avoided for so long.

Chapter 8: Confronting Themselves

Yin and Yang stood before their mirrored reflections, the air thick with tension. The dark and light counterparts seemed alive, their voices cutting through the silence like whispers of truth they had long avoided.

Her glowing double tilted its head, a serene yet piercing gaze locking onto her. You're afraid of your own strength, Yin. You hide behind your gentleness, thinking it makes you good, but sometimes gentleness is just fear in disguise.

Yin felt her chest tighten. I'm not afraid of my strength. I just don't want to hurt anyone.

Then why do you always hesitate? the reflection countered. Why do you let others decide for you, waiting for the right moment that never comes?

I... I don't know, Yin admitted, her voice cracking.

You do know, the reflection pressed. You fear what happens when your power goes unchecked. But balance isn't about holding back; it's about control. Find your strength, Yin. Embrace it.

Yang's dark reflection smirked, circling her like a predator. You think you're tough because you fight first and think later, but it's not strength it's avoidance. You're scared of being vulnerable, scared of letting anyone in.

That's not true! Yang snapped; her fists clenched.

Isn't it? the reflection asked. Why do you always push people away when things get hard? Why do you protect Yin like she's your crutch, instead of trusting her to protect herself?

Yang froze, the words hitting harder than she expected. I protect her because she's, my sister.

You protect her because you're afraid of being alone, the reflection corrected. Admit it, Yang. You don't trust anyone, not even yourself.

Yang's voice softened. I... I don't know how to trust. Not fully.

Then learn, the reflection said, stepping closer. Strength isn't just about fighting. It's about standing still when everything in you says to run.

As Yin and Yang absorbed the truths revealed by their reflections, the mirrored figures began to dissolve, leaving behind a faint glow of light and shadow. The twins turned to each other; their gazes heavy with understanding.

I've been holding back, Yin admitted. Afraid of what I might do.

And I've been pushing too hard, Yang said. Afraid of what happens if I don't.

They reached out, clasping hands. We've got this, they said in unison, their voices steady.

The node pulsed with energy, stabilizing as the balance within them shifted.

Rising Tensions on Earth

Back on Earth, Jason, Elijah, and Tasha tried to make sense of the strange occurrences that had started spreading beyond just Tasha. Small blackouts, random levitations, and unexplained energy surges were becoming more frequent.

I don't think this is just about the twins anymore, Elijah said, watching a flickering streetlight. Something bigger is happening.

Jason frowned. If they don't fix it, what happens to the rest of us?

I'll tell you what happens, Tasha said, her voice sharp. This whole world falls apart. And I'm not about to let that happen.

Jason raised an eyebrow. What do you suggest? We can't exactly jump into whatever realm they're in.

Tasha's eyes glinted with determination. Maybe not, but we can figure out where the next disruption will be. If we can find the pattern, we can be there when they return and maybe even help.

Elijah hesitated. You're talking about tracking energy nodes on Earth. That's... complicated.

Not if you have someone who can sense them, Tasha said, holding up her hand as a faint spark of light danced across her fingertips.

Jason's eyes widened. You can feel them?

I don't know how, Tasha admitted. But ever since that night, it's like I'm connected to something bigger. If they won't tell us what's going on, then we'll find out ourselves.

As the twins emerged from the second node, they felt a ripple of unease. The balance in their world was shifting, but the disturbances on Earth were growing stronger.

Do you feel that? Yang asked.

Yeah, Yin said. Something's wrong back home.

They exchanged a glance. It was time to return to Earth.

Chapter 9: The Return

Yin and Yang stood on the edge of the rift between realms, the swirling energy of their celestial world fading as Earth came into view. The transition was jarring bright lights, faint sirens, and the unmistakable hum of human life surrounded them. But something felt... off.

The twins appeared on a quiet street near their home, their arrival marked by a crackle of energy. Before they could take a step, Jason and Elijah's car screeched to a halt in front of them.

Jason jumped out, his face a mixture of relief and disbelief. Yin! Yang!

Elijah followed close behind, staring at them as if they might vanish again. You're... you're here.

The twins exchanged a look, a small smile tugging at Yang's lips. Told you we wouldn't be gone forever.

Jason approached cautiously, his voice trembling. Nine months. Do you even realize how long you've been gone?

Yin's smile faltered. We know. And we're sorry. But we had to go. Things were... complicated.

Complicated doesn't even begin to cover it, Elijah said, crossing his arms. Do you have any idea what's been happening here? The power surges, the blackouts, the

Levitation? Yang interrupted, smirking.

Jason's eyes widened. You knew?

Sort of, Yin admitted. It's connected to us. To what we are. Before they could explain further, another voice cut through the tension. And what exactly *are* you?

The group turned to see Tasha stepping out of the shadows, her expression unreadable. Jason instinctively moved closer to Yin, while Yang's posture stiffened.

Tasha, Yin said cautiously. This isn't the time for

For what? Questions? Answers? Tasha interrupted, holding up her hand as sparks of light danced along her fingertips. You're not the only ones changing, you know. Ever since prom night, I've been... different. And it's because of you two.

The twins exchanged a wary glance.

She's not lying, Elijah said. She's been sensing energy disruptions all over town. She helped us track down where you might come back.

Tasha crossed her arms. So, are you going to explain what's happening, or do I have to figure it out myself?

Yang sighed. Fine. But not here. Let's go somewhere quiet.

The group gathered in the twins' living room, the once familiar space now filled with an undercurrent of unease. Yin and Yang sat across from Jason, Elijah, and Tasha, their expressions serious.

We weren't just gone, Yin began. We were... learning. About ourselves, our powers, and our connection to the universe.

Yang continued, We're part of something bigger. Guardians of balance between realms. And Earth is at the center of it all.

Tasha frowned. Guardians? Balance? That still doesn't explain why I'm suddenly zapping lightbulbs every time I get mad.

The disruptions on Earth are a side effect, Yin explained. When we left, it created an imbalance. People like you those who were close to the energy nodes became conduits for that energy.

Jason leaned forward. So, what now? How do we fix it?

We must restore the balance, Yang said. But it's not just about Earth. The entire universe is connected. If one realm falls out of balance, it affects everything. Tasha's eyes narrowed. And what happens if you fail?

Yin hesitated. Then Earth and everything else might not survive.

As the night went on, the weight of their roles began to settle on the twins. While the others discussed plans and strategies, Yin and Yang retreated to their room, the familiar space offering little comfort.

This isn't going to be easy, Yin said, sitting on her bed.

It never is, Yang replied, leaning against the wall. But we've got each other. And now, we've got them too.

Yin nodded, her gaze distant. I just hope it's enough.

Meanwhile, as the group debated their next steps, a ripple of dark energy swept through the town. Shadows began to stir in places they shouldn't, and a low hum echoed through the air, almost like a heartbeat.

Far away, in the remnants of the prom night gym, a figure emerged from the darkness. Its form was indistinct, shifting between shadow and light, but its intent was clear.

They've returned, it whispered, its voice a chilling echo. And so shall we.

Chapter 10: Personal Struggles

The twins' return to Earth was supposed to be a fresh start, but it was quickly turning into a test of their strength and resolve. Balancing their cosmic responsibilities with the weight of their personal lives was proving to be more difficult than they had imagined.

Yin found herself drawn to Jason more than ever, but the newfound weight of her responsibilities created an invisible wall between them. One evening, as they sat on her front porch under the soft glow of the moon, Jason finally broke the silence.

You've been quiet since you came back, he said, leaning against the porch railing. What's going on in that head of yours?

Yin hesitated. It's hard to explain. Everything feels... bigger now. Like I'm not just Yin anymore. I'm something more, and it scares me.

Jason reached out, gently taking her hand. You don't have to do this alone. I'm here, no matter what.

Yin smiled faintly, but there was a flicker of doubt in her eyes. I just don't want you to get hurt.

Jason's voice was steady. I'd rather stand by your side and face whatever comes than sit on the sidelines and lose you again.

Yang, on the other hand, was wrestling with her sense of independence. She had always been the more confident and outgoing twin, but the events in the celestial realm had shaken her. Sitting in her room one night, she confided in Elijah.

What if we're not enough? she asked, her voice barely above a whisper.

Elijah, sitting cross legged on her bed, tilted his head. Enough for what?

For this, she said, gesturing vaguely. The balance, the universe, all of it. What if we fail?

Elijah's laugh was soft but genuine. Yang, you're the most determined person I know. You don't fail. You adapt, you fight, and you win. That's who you are.

Yang chuckled despite herself. You really know how to make a girl feel better.

Elijah grinned. It's a talent.

As the twins worked to rebuild their relationships, the mysterious disturbances around town began to escalate. Lights flickered, unnatural winds howled, and whispers carried on the breeze.

One afternoon, Tasha burst into the twins' house unannounced, her eyes wide with panic.

You guys need to see this, she said, dragging them to her car.

She drove them to the remnants of the old gym, where the prom disaster had unfolded. The space was eerily silent, but the walls were now marked with strange symbols that seemed to pulse with a faint, dark light.

What is this? Yang asked, running her fingers over one of the symbols.

Tasha shook her head. I don't know, but they weren't here yesterday. And look.

She pointed to the floor, where a pool of dark energy rippled like liquid shadow. Yin knelt, her hand hovering over it.

It's familiar, she said, her voice low.

It's them, Yang added, her jaw tightening. The ones who tried to stop us before. They're back.

As if summoned by their words, the pool of shadow began to rise, taking shape into a humanoid figure cloaked in darkness. Its eyes glowed with a cold, pale light.

Guardians, it hissed, its voice like wind through dead leaves. You should have stayed away.

Yang stepped forward, her fists clenched. And miss out on the fun? Not a chance.

The figure chuckled darkly. Your arrogance will be your undoing.

Before anyone could react, it lunged toward Yin. Jason and Elijah, who had followed them to the gym, stepped in front of her without hesitation. Elijah raised his hands, instinctively creating a barrier of light that repelled the creature.

What the Elijah stared at his glowing hands in shock.

Yang grabbed his arm. We'll explain later. For now, keep doing that!

Yin focused her energy, summoning a wave of starlight that struck the figure, forcing it to retreat. But before it vanished, it left them with a chilling warning.

The balance is broken, and the void is rising. Your world will fall.

After the encounter, the group regrouped at the twins' house. Tasha paced nervously, while Jason and Elijah sat quietly, still processing what had happened.

We need to figure out what they're after, Yang said, her voice firm.

And why they're targeting Earth specifically, Yin added.

Tasha crossed her arms. Well, whatever it is, they clearly don't want you two here. Which means you're the key to stopping them.

Jason nodded. Then we fight. Together.

Elijah smiled faintly. Guess we're part of this now, whether we like it or not.

Yin and Yang exchanged a determined look. Then let's do this, Yin said. We stopped them once. We can do it again.

But deep down, they both knew this time would be different. The stakes were higher, and the enemy was stronger.

And the void was rising.

Chapter 11: Training and the Rising Void

The calm before the storm was always the hardest to bear. The group spent days preparing, both physically and emotionally, for the battle ahead. Yin and Yang, despite their immense power, knew they needed to refine their abilities especially if they were going to face the true magnitude of the darkness that was slowly creeping into their world.

In a secluded area of the forest, far from prying eyes, Yin and Yang stood side by side, with Jason, Elijah, and Tasha watching from a distance. The sun was beginning to set, casting an orange glow over the horizon, creating the perfect atmosphere for their training.

Yang stretched, feeling the tension in her body. She knew she had the power, but controlling it was something entirely different.

You ready? Yin asked, her voice calm but serious.

As ready as I'll ever be, Yang replied, a glint of determination in her eyes.

Good. Let's start with control, Yin instructed. Focus on your core. Let the energy flow through you, but don't let it overwhelm you.

Yang closed her eyes, feeling the pulse of her energy, her connection to the universe. She reached deep within, trying to harness the dark energy without letting it consume her. It wasn't easy. The force inside her was wild, like a tempest waiting to be unleashed.

I can feel it. It's like the power wants to break free, Yang admitted, frustration lining her voice.

Yin nodded. It does. But you must guide it. If you let it loose without control, it could destroy everything.

Yang exhaled deeply, trying again. This time, she focused on her breathing, grounding herself before she attempted to channel the dark energy into a coherent form. Slowly, she raised her hand, and dark tendrils of energy began to swirl around her fingers, twisting and weaving. The energy flickered like lightning.

Good, Yin said, stepping closer. Now, push it outward. Channel it into a blast.

Yang thrust her hand forward, and a wave of dark energy shot out, crashing into a nearby tree, splintering it into pieces. The shockwave sent a ripple through the ground.

Not bad, Yin said with a smirk. But remember, your control is what will win the battle. You can't let it destroy you, Yang.

Yang nodded, sweat dripping down her face. She knew Yin was right. There was more at stake now than ever before.

Meanwhile, Jason and Elijah were also pushing their limits. Elijah, with his newfound ability to manipulate light, was still learning how to create barriers and attacks that could hold back the shadows. Jason had a different challenge. He had no celestial connection with the twins, but his bond with Yin had unlocked something within him a strength that wasn't there before.

You're doing good, bro, Elijah said, watching Jason focus. You've got power in you. Just keep honing it.

Jason nodded but didn't take his eyes off the training ground. He focused on the space between his hands, trying to summon energy. It wasn't easy, but he could feel something building. Slowly, a soft blue light flickered between his fingers, like a flame struggling to stay lit in the wind.

That's it. You've got it, Elijah encouraged.

Jason's brow furrowed. It's weak. I need more. I need to help Yin and Yang.

You will. You just need to trust in your own strength. Don't rely on theirs. Your connection with them makes you powerful, but it's you who must wield it.

Jason took a deep breath. He pushed harder, feeling his energy align with his intent. The light grew brighter, more focused, until it pulsed with intensity. He shot his hand forward, releasing a blast of blue light that sent a nearby rock flying.

Now that's what I'm talking about, Elijah said with a grin. You're getting it. Just remember, it's all about focus.
As the team trained, the disturbance in the world around them grew more pronounced. It wasn't just strange phenomena anymore people began to disappear, cities were plagued with power outages, and strange creatures

appeared in the night. The void was not only a threat to their world but seemed to be eating away at the fabric of reality itself.

Yin and Yang began to feel the pull of the void more intensely. Every night, they had vivid dreams of a vast, swirling darkness. Sometimes, they could hear voices from the shadows whispers of ancient entities that wanted nothing more than to engulf the universe in darkness.

I don't know how much longer we can keep it at bay, Yin said one evening, her voice filled with worry as she and Yang sat on the porch, watching the stars flicker overhead.

Then we'll face it head on, Yang replied. We must. We can't wait any longer.

Yin nodded, determination in her eyes. Let's do this.

Preparing for the Final Battle

With each passing day, their training grew more intense. The bond between Yin and Yang, already unbreakable, grew stronger as they learned to channel their power together. Jason, Elijah, and Tasha worked tirelessly to improve their own abilities, knowing they would need every ounce of strength to help the twins.

The final battle was approaching. The group gathered one last time in the forest, their faces grim but resolute.

We'll face the darkness, together, Yang said, her voice steady and filled with purpose.

Yin looked to the horizon, where the first signs of the void were beginning to appear, like a dark storm on the horizon. This is it. The time has come.

With their powers united, the group prepared to face the void and its mysterious forces. The future of their world and the universe was hanging in the balance.

Chapter 12: The Confrontation with the Void

The atmosphere around them was heavy. The trees in the forest rustled with an unnatural wind, and the sky had darkened to a deep shade of purple, as though the very heavens themselves were holding their breath. The group stood at the edge of the clearing, their nerves taut with anticipation. Yin, Yang, Jason, Elijah, and Tasha were ready, but they knew the fight they were about to face was unlike anything they had ever experienced. It wasn't just a physical battle it was a battle for the soul of their world.

The Void was coming, and it was far more than just an entity. It was an ancient force, a consuming darkness that devoured everything in its path. It had no form, no shape, only an endless hunger for destruction.

As the wind howled louder, the ground beneath them trembled. The void was nearby.

Yin and Yang stepped forward, their hands glowing faintly with dark and light energy. They could feel the pulse of the Void vibrating in the air, the very fabric of reality bending and warping. It was an oppressive, suffocating force that threatened to overwhelm them.

We've never faced anything like this before, Yin said, her voice low, her eyes scanning the horizon. But I feel it. It's here.

Yang clenched her fists, the dark energy swirling around her. We must stop it, or we'll lose everything.

Jason, standing beside them, could feel the hairs on the back of his neck stand up. How do we fight something like this? It's not just physical... it's something deeper.

Yin turned to him, her expression grave. You fight it with everything you have. Your strength, your heart, your connection to us. The Void feeds on fear, on weakness. If we stand united, we can hold it back. But we need to be strong... together.

Elijah stepped forward, his light powers radiating from him like a beacon. Let's be clear, though. This isn't just about stopping the Void. It's about protecting our world. The darkness wants to erase everything our memories, our relationships, even the stars in the sky. We can't let that happen.

Tasha stood by her face determined. I'm ready, too. We all are.

With a shared, resolute glance, they turned their attention back to the horizon. The ground before them cracked, and the air grew colder. The first visible manifestation of the Void emerged a swirling mass of shadows that stretched and writhed like a living entity.

The Battle Begins

The air crackled with energy as the Void materialized, its immense presence warping the world around it. The darkness swirled and coiled, it's very essence a corrupting, inescapable pull. The earth beneath their feet began to crack and splinter as the Void's energy grew stronger, seeping into the ground.

Stay focused! Yang shouted. The more we let it affect us, the more it will consume!

Yin raised her hand, and dark energy erupted in the form of tendrils that shot toward the Void. The shadows tried to twist around her power, but she forced them back, her energy crackling with intensity.

Jason stood beside her, his blue light illuminating the darkness. We can do this. We're together. He focused, summoning his energy. The blue light shot from his palms in waves, creating barriers of protection against the encroaching shadows.

Elijah's light power was even stronger now. His hands glowed like the sun, casting golden beams into the night as he summoned pillars of light to push back the dark. We must keep it contained! If we let it get any bigger

Before he could finish, a massive wave of darkness surged forward, crashing against their defenses. The ground trembled beneath them, and they could feel the pull of the Void trying to tear them apart.

Get ready! Yin shouted. We need to combine our powers.

The twins stood in the center of the battlefield, their powers swirling around them. The Void was unlike any enemy they had ever faced it wasn't just an external force, but an internal one, preying on their deepest fears, their vulnerabilities. But it was in their shared bond, in their connection, that they found their strength.

Yin reached out her hand to Yang, and the two connected their energy. The dark energy and light energy merged, creating a pulse of raw power that rippled through the air. Their combined energy became a force of nature something more powerful than either could create alone.

We must close it, Yang said, her voice steady despite the chaos around them.

I know, Yin replied. We do it together. Let's end this.

With a shared, unspoken understanding, the twins lifted their arms toward the sky. The merging energies created a swirling vortex of both light and dark that spiraled upward, forming a massive dome around them.

The Void resisted, its tendrils reaching toward the twins, but the light and darkness that came from their combined strength burned like a cleansing fire.

You won't win, Yin said, her eyes glowing with intensity. We are the balance. You cannot break us.

The Void screeched, a sound that tore at the very fabric of the universe. But the more they focused, the more they poured their energy into the vortex, the more the Void began to crumble. The darkness writhed in pain as the energy from the twins enveloped it, breaking it apart piece by piece.

As the Void began to collapse, a sudden surge of darkness erupted from the center, attempting to consume the twins' energy. It felt like a final, desperate attempt to break their connection and destroy everything.

No! Yang cried out, her hands trembling as she fought to maintain the connection. We can't let it win.

Jason ran toward them, his blue light intensifying. Yin! Yang! We've got your backs! He thrust his hands forward, sending a wave of energy to reinforce their attack.

Tasha, too, jumped in, her presence more powerful than ever. With her celestial abilities, her unwavering support and determination became a vital part of the team's strength. With a final, united push, the twins locked their hands together, forcing all their energy into the void. The darkness trembled, then cracked, shattering into millions of tiny fragments that dissolved into nothingness.

The Aftermath

The sky cleared, and the oppressive darkness lifted. The ground beneath them, once cracked and dying, began to heal. The air felt lighter, the oppressive weight lifted. They had done it. They had defeated the Void.

But as the battle subsided, the group was left in stunned silence. It was over... but at what cost?

Yin and Yang stood side by side, their energy depleted, but their bond stronger than ever. Jason and Elijah, breathing heavily, shared a look of relief, while Tasha, though exhausted, smiled. The universe was safe for now.

We did it, Yin whispered, her voice hoarse from the battle. But there's still so much more to understand. The Void may be gone, but it's not the end. There are more questions... more answers we need.

Yang nodded; her face determined. And we'll face them. Together.

The team stood in the quiet aftermath, united, knowing that their journey was far from over but for the first time in a long time, they were ready for whatever came next.

Chapter 13: Aftermath and New Beginnings

The battle with the Void had left its mark on all of them. The energy was still thick in the air, lingering like the aftermath of a storm. The world around them had healed, but the emotional scars of what they had endured would take longer to fade.

As the first light of dawn broke through the horizon, the group gathered on the edge of the forest. They were physically drained, but the bond between them was stronger than it had ever been. Yin and Yang stood together, their hands still tingling with the combined energy they had used to defeat the Void. Jason, Elijah, and Tasha surrounded them, each one with their own thoughts swirling in the quiet aftermath of the battle.

Jason had always been there for Yin, but the battle had forced them both to confront the complexities of their relationship. The tension between them had been thick, and for a moment, Yin had doubted whether they could truly move past the misunderstandings and emotional chaos that had been building for months.

Jason looked at Yin, his hazel eyes reflecting a mixture of concern and love. He walked over to her, his voice tentative but filled with sincerity.

Yin, he said softly. I... I don't know how to explain all of this. Everything we went through, everything I did wrong... I just

Yin turned to him, her face tired but resolute. She could see the weight of everything Jason had been carrying.

Jason, I don't need explanations, she said, her voice steady. We've both made mistakes. We've both hurt each other. But I know what I feel, and I know that... whatever this is, whatever we are... it's worth fighting for. If you're still willing to fight, then so am I.

Jason took a step closer, reaching for her hand. The tension between them began to dissolve as their connection rekindled, and Yin felt the last of her doubts dissipate.

I'm sorry, he whispered, his grip tightening around her hand. I love you.

Yin smiled softly. I love you too, Jason.

Yang had always been the more guarded of the twins, and the events of the battle had forced her to confront not just the darkness of the Void but also her own inner fears. She had often buried her emotions under a tough exterior, but the intensity of the battle had cracked that shell. Standing next to Elijah, she realized that there was more than just a connection between them; there was an understanding that went beyond words.

Elijah, still reeling from the intensity of the battle, stood quietly beside her, sensing the shift in her energy. He had always respected her space, but in that moment, he could feel the raw vulnerability in her that she usually kept hidden.

Yang, he said softly, turning to her. We've been through a lot, huh?

Yang smiled, though there was a sadness in her eyes. Yeah, a lot more than I ever expected. She looked up at him, and for the first time, the walls she had built around herself began to crumble. I've never been good at this... at letting people in. But with you, I don't feel like I have to hold back.

Elijah reached out, gently brushing a strand of hair from her face. You don't have to. Not with me.

Their connection had always been there, unspoken, but now it was something more. It was real, raw, and honest. The fight had stripped away their doubts, and now there was nothing between them but the truth.

I think I've been waiting for you to say that Yang whispered, her voice barely audible.

Elijah smiled, pulling her closer. I've been right here, waiting for you to see it.

They stood in silence for a moment, just being together. The world around them had changed and so had their relationship. It was no longer just a bond of convenience or shared adventure. It was something deeper, something that neither of them could deny.

Tasha: Redemption and Self-Acceptance

Tasha had been on a journey of her own. The battle against the Void had been more than just a physical confrontation for her it had been a wakeup call. Her jealousy, her bitterness, and the wounds from the past had all been exposed during the battle, and as she stood among the group, she knew that the real fight was still ahead of her. Not against the Void, but against herself.

As she watched Yin and Jason, Yang and Elijah, something stirred within her. For the first time, she saw what true connection looked like. It wasn't just about being with someone because of status or appearance; it was about love, trust, and vulnerability.

She had spent so much time trying to tear others down to build herself up, but now she saw that the only way to truly grow was to heal.

Tasha turned to Yin and Yang, her voice low but sincere. I don't expect forgiveness. But I want to thank you. For everything. For showing me that I need to change. I'm not proud of who I've been.

Yin looked at her, a flicker of understanding in her eyes. You don't need to be perfect, Tasha. You just need to try. That's all any of us can do.

Yang nodded; her face softened. We all have our battles. You've fought yours, and now you're choosing to be better. That's what matters.

Tasha smiled faintly, the weight of her past no longer as heavy as it once was. She had a long road ahead of her, but for the first time in a long time, she felt like she was on the right path.

As the group stood together, the world around them was healing. The Void had been vanquished, but they knew that the universe still held mysteries, still held threats that would one day come. But now, they were stronger not just because of the powers they wielded, but because of the trust they had in one another.

Yin and Yang had become more than just sisters; they had become the anchors of their world. They were no longer simply bearers of cosmic power. They were the balance of light and dark, the protectors of their realm, and the guardians of their relationships.

The journey was far from over, but the storm that had once threatened to consume them had passed. They had faced the Void and emerged victorious, but more importantly, they had faced themselves and in doing so, they had forged bonds that could never be broken.

Yin took one last look at the horizon, feeling a deep sense of peace settle within her. She didn't know what the future held, but for the first time, she felt ready to face it.

I think we've earned a little peace, don't you? Yin said, her voice filled with hope.

Yang smiled. Yeah. But the adventures just begun.

And with that, the twins walked forward into the unknown, knowing that whatever challenges awaited them, they would face them together stronger than ever before.

The End